EDGE BOOKS™

TRUE TALES OF SURVIVAL PRESENTS:

SHARK ATTACK!

BETHANY HAMILTON'S STORY OF SURVIVAL

by Tim O'Shei

Consultant:
Al Siebert, PhD
Author of *The Survivor Personality*

Capstone press®

Mankato, Minnesota

7/07

Edge Books are published by Capstone Press,
151 Good Counsel Drive, P.O. Box 669, Mankato, Minnesota 56002.
www.capstonepress.com

Library of Congress Cataloging-in-Publication Data
Doeden, Matt.
    Shark attack!: Bethany Hamilton's story of suvival / by Matt Doeden.
    p. cm.—(Edge books. True tales of survival)
    Includes bibliographical references and index.
    Summary:"Describes how 13-year old surfer Bethany Hamily survived an
attack by a tiger shark that took her left arm."—provided by publisher.
    ISBN-13: 978-0-7368-6776-4 (hardcover)
    ISBN-10: 0-7368-6776-7 (hardcover)
    ISBN-13: 978-0-7368-7866-1 (softcover pbk.)
    ISBN-10: 0-7368-7866-1 (softcover pbk.)
    1. Hamilton, Bethany. 2. Surfing—Hawaii—Kauai—Accidents and injuries. 3.
Shark attacks—Hawaii—Kauai. 4. Amputees—Rehabilitation. I. Title. II. Series.

GV838.H36D64 2007
797.3'209969   2006032887

Editorial Credits
Mandy Robbins, editor; Jason Knudson, designer; Wanda Winch, photo
    researcher/photo editor

Photo Credits
Brand X Pictures, 22–23 (background), 30–31 (background), 32 (background)
Comstock, 1 (background)
Corbis/Frank Trapper, 20; Macduff Everton, 4–5; Nancy Kaszerman, 24; Royalty-
    Free, 18–19 (background)
Creatas, 2–3 (background), 14–15 (background), 28–29 (background)
Digital Vision, 16–17 (background)
Getty Images Inc./Giulio Marcocchi, 19 (top); Kevin Winter, 25; Scott Gries, 23
Honolulu Advertiser, The/Richard Ambo, 12–13, 14–15
Jeff Rotman, cover, 19 (bottom)
SeaPics.com/Doug Perrine, 8–9
Shutterstock, back cover; Merrill Dyck, 20–21 (background)
Zuma Press/A-Frame/Brian Nevins, 10–11; Jon Steele, 26–27; KPA/Rena Durham,16;
    Robert Kenney, 29; The Garden Island/D. Fujimoto, 6–7

1 2 3 4 5 6 12 11 10 09 08 07

TABLE OF CONTENTS

CHAPTER 1

FROM PEACE TO PANIC

LEARN ABOUT:

- AN ORDINARY DAY
- CALM BLUE OCEAN
- SUDDEN TERROR

4

Bethany Hamilton happily floated on a surfboard. The sun sparkled on Tunnels Beach, Hawaii. It was around 7:00 in the morning.

Surfing was 13-year-old Bethany's passion. She enjoyed the sand, the water, and the sun. She loved the rush of riding a big wave.

Bethany didn't realize that her life was about to change forever.

5

To her left, Bethany noticed something creeping beneath the water. It was large and gray. It lurked slowly and silently. But Bethany wasn't scared. She was used to sharing the ocean with other creatures. Bethany didn't realize that her life was about to change forever.

In an instant, the calm blue ocean burst into a splash of white water. The creature below the surface charged at Bethany. A nearby surfer thought he heard a scream.

EDGE FACT

A child surfer is called a "grom."

When Bethany was in the ocean, her thoughts were on the waves, not sharks.

CHAPTER 2

NATURAL-BORN SURFER

LEARN ABOUT:
- A FAMILY SPORT
- SHARPENING HER SKILLS
- CHASING DREAMS

8

The island of Kauai has more than 50 miles (80 kilometers) of beaches.

Bethany grew up on the Hawaiian island of Kauai. Surfing is the island's most popular sport. Many children start learning to surf when they are toddlers.

The island of Kauai has lots of beaches and great waves. In the 1970s, many surfers from the mainland moved there to enjoy the sand and surf. Bethany's parents were among them. It was on Kauai's sandy beaches that the two surfers met. Bethany's father, Tom Hamilton, is from New Jersey. Her mother, Cheri, is from California. After getting married, Tom and Cheri had two sons, Noah and Timothy. Bethany, their third child, was born February 8, 1990.

A SURFING FAMILY

Tom and Cheri taught their children to surf when they were very young. Bethany started learning at age 5. She was a natural. At age 7, Bethany was surfing without her parents' help. By the time Bethany was 11, she was a serious competitive surfer. She was also being home schooled so that she had more time to practice surfing.

Tom and Cheri encouraged Bethany to follow her surfing dreams. Tom was a hotel waiter, and Cheri occasionally worked as a banquet waitress. They entered Bethany in competitions, and somehow found the money to pay the related expenses. Competition also meant traveling. Airline tickets, hotel rooms, and restaurant bills were expensive. But Bethany's parents managed to keep her competing.

Bethany's parents supported her surfing dreams in every way possible.

11

By the time she was 13, Bethany had surfed in 200 competitions. Rip Curl, a surfing company, agreed to sponsor Bethany. As her sponsor, Rip Curl paid all of her competition expenses.

Surfing experts thought Bethany was a rising star.

Bethany kept improving. In 2003, she finished second in the U.S. under-18 surfing championship. There were only about 25 professional female surfers in the world. Surfing experts believed Bethany would soon be one of them.

CHAPTER 3

A VIOLENT ATTACK

14

The tiger shark that bit Bethany took a chunk out of her surfboard as well.

LEARN ABOUT:

- **A HALLOWEEN SCARE**
- **EMERGENCY SURGERY**
- **OVERWHELMING SUPPORT**

On Halloween 2003, Cheri woke Bethany around 5:00 in the morning and asked, "Wanna go surfing?" Of course, Bethany answered yes. This was the usual way to start her day.

Cheri took Bethany to Tunnels Beach. At the beach, Bethany ran into her friend, Alana Blanchard. Alana was at the beach with her father, Holt, and brother, Byron. Cheri left Bethany to surf with the Blanchards.

Bethany and the Blanchards surfed for about half an hour. None of them guessed what would happen next.

15

Bethany had noticed the large gray figure under the water. But she never got a good look at it. A tiger shark the length of a minivan burst out of the water. It clamped its jaws onto Bethany's left arm. Instead of pain, she felt a "jiggle-jiggle-tug." Then the shark disappeared under the water. A chunk of Bethany's surfboard was missing. So was her left arm.

SURVIVAL INSTINCT

"I got attacked by a shark," Bethany shouted to Alana, who was swimming nearby. Bethany was not panicked. She was just focused on getting out of the water. When facing a deadly situation, some people ignore pain and focus on simply staying alive. Scientists call this the survival instinct.

The shore was about 200 yards (180 meters) away. Holt and Byron swam to Bethany to help her get back to the beach. Holt took off his T-shirt and tied it around Bethany's wound. He used a rubber surf leash as a tourniquet. He hoped it would stop Bethany from bleeding too much. Later, a doctor said that Holt's quick actions saved Bethany's life.

An ambulance rushed Bethany to Wilcox Memorial Hospital. A man at Tunnels Beach called Cheri to tell her what had happened. Terrified, she called her sons to tell them the news. All three Hamiltons headed to the hospital.

17

> **Tom had a bad feeling that the victim was either Bethany or Alana.**

SURGERY SWITCH

Tom Hamilton was already at the hospital, though he had no idea that his daughter had been hurt. Tom was in an operating room, preparing for minor surgery on his leg. A nurse burst into the room and told the doctor that a 13-year-old girl had been attacked by a shark. Tom had a bad feeling that the victim was either Bethany or Alana.

The doctor left the room to find out more information. Five minutes later, he returned. With tears in his eyes, the doctor told Tom the bite victim was Bethany. Tom was wheeled out of the operating room. The doctors needed it to operate on his daughter.

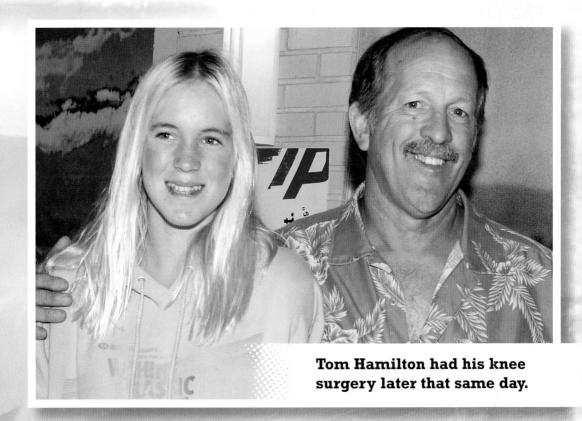

Tom Hamilton had his knee surgery later that same day.

The shark that bit Bethany was a 14-foot (4-meter) long tiger shark.

Bethany has a thin curved
scar where the doctors
stitched up her wound.

BETHANY IS BIG NEWS

The biggest dangers with shark-bite injuries are losing blood and getting infections. During Bethany's six days in the hospital, doctors gave her blood transfusions. They also watched her wound closely to make sure it wasn't getting infected.

Meanwhile, flowers and balloons flooded Bethany's hospital room. Reporters caught word of the attack too. Soon, stories about Bethany's attack appeared in newspapers and on TV shows around the world.

After two surgeries, doctors stitched Bethany's wound closed. Only a small stump of her arm remained.

As Bethany left the hospital, she prayed that her surfing career wasn't over. But with only one arm, she knew it would be difficult to get back on a surfboard again.

CHAPTER 4

ROAD TO RECOVERY

LEARN ABOUT:
- INSTANT CELEBRITY
- NEW OPPORTUNITIES
- BACK ON BOARD

22

The Hamiltons did not take Bethany home when she left the hospital. Reporters were camping out at their house, trying to get a story. At home there would be no privacy and no chance to rest.

The family stayed at a friend's home in Anahola Beach. The Hamiltons' family friend, Roy Hofstetter, managed all interview requests. One day, each interviewer got three minutes to ask Bethany questions in the living room.

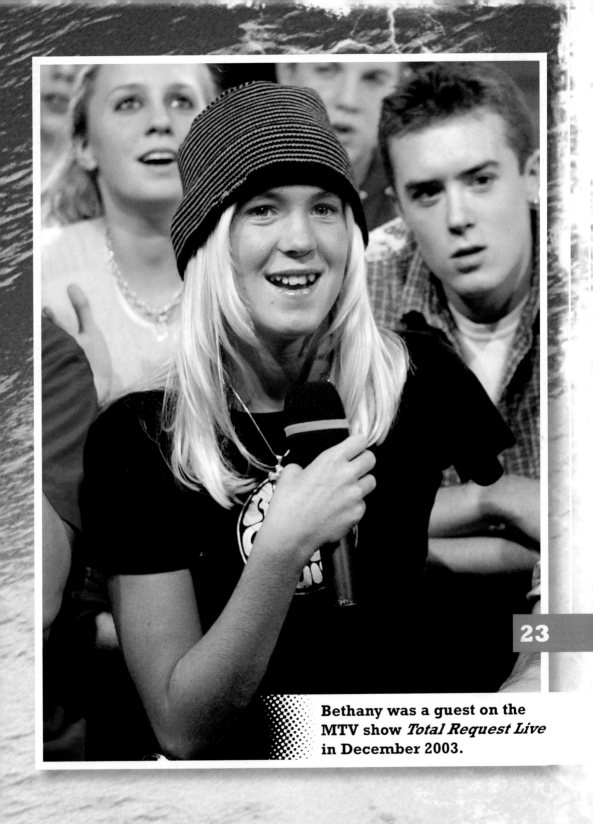

23

Bethany was a guest on the MTV show *Total Request Live* in December 2003.

Bethany promotes two lines of perfume. *Stoked* is for girls, and *Wired* is for boys.

In the months that followed, Bethany became a celebrity. She hired an agent, wrote a book, and made plans for a movie about her life. She was a guest on dozens of TV and radio shows. Her story appeared in hundreds of magazines and newspapers. Companies hired her to promote products ranging from perfume to juice drinks.

24

Bethany often made an extra effort to talk to people with physical challenges. She also became involved with charities that help people with physical challenges.

Bethany had mixed feelings about the constant attention. When asked how she felt about it, she used the words "fun," "annoying," "exciting," and "boring." All she really wanted to do was surf.

Bethany won a 2004 Teen Choice Award for her courage.

25

Less than one month after her injury, Bethany showed people that she wouldn't stop pursuing her goal. On Thanksgiving Day 2003, she returned to the ocean, surfboard in hand. With her family and Alana watching, Bethany tried to surf again. With only one arm, she had to paddle and balance differently. Her first attempts failed. But her father called out, "Bethany, try it one more time. This one will be it!" In no time, Bethany was on her board, riding the waves.

EDGE FACT

Bethany is a "goofy-foot" surfer. She puts her right foot in front on a surfboard, while most surfers put their left foot in front.

Bethany returned to competitive surfing just 10 weeks after the attack.

In the following weeks, Bethany continued to improve. She soon returned to competition and regained her reputation as one of the world's best young female surfers.

Almost a year later, a group of kids interviewed Bethany. One of them asked her about her first time back on a surfboard. Bethany admitted that she cried, but not out of sadness. These were tears of joy.

EDGE FACT

When Bethany first lost her arm, she thought she would never surf again. Instead she wanted to become a surfing photographer.

Bethany's book, *Soul Surfer*, was published in 2004.

GLOSSARY

agent (AY-juhnt)—someone who arranges things for other people; Bethany's agent arranges television, magazine, and newspaper interviews for her.

infection (in-FEK-shuhn)—an illness caused by germs growing in the body

mainland (MAIN-land)—the name Hawaiians have for the 48 continental states of the United States

tourniquet (TURN-i-ket)—a tight wrapping designed to prevent a major loss of blood

transfusion (trans-FEW-shun)—the act of transferring blood into a person

wound (WOOND)—an injury or cut

READ MORE

Hamilton, Bethany. *Soul Surfer.* New York: Pocket Books; MTV Books, 2004.

O'Shei, Tim. *The World's Most Amazing Survival Stories.* The World's Top Tens. Mankato, Minn.: Capstone Press, 2007.

Tihanyi, Izzy, and Coco Tihanyi. *Surf Diva: A Girl's Guide to Getting Good Waves.* Orlando: Harcourt, 2005.

INTERNET SITES

FactHound offers a safe, fun way to find Internet sites related to this book. All of the sites on FactHound have been researched by our staff.

Here's how:

1. Visit *www.facthound.com*

2. Choose your grade level.

3. Type in this book ID **0736867767** for age-appropriate sites. You may also browse subjects by clicking on letters, or by clicking on pictures and words.

4. Click on the **Fetch It** button.

FactHound will fetch the best sites for you!

INDEX